BE A LEADER

LEADERSHIP AT HOME

BY JAMES HANCOCK

BLUE OWL
BOOKS

TIPS FOR CAREGIVERS

Leadership can be an intimidating and abstract concept. Finding ways to encourage small, everyday examples of leadership can help instill the traits of a good leader in young readers. It is important to know that there are many leadership traits, forms of leadership, and types of leaders. By helping young people identify all of the possibilities, you can help them find which types of leaders they want to be. Learning how to demonstrate the traits of a leader is a form of social and emotional learning (SEL).

BEFORE READING

Talk to the reader about leadership.

Discuss: What does leadership mean to you? Who are some leaders in your life? How do they lead?

AFTER READING

Talk to the reader about how he or she can practice leadership.

Discuss: What can you do at home to practice different types of leadership?

SEL GOAL

Young readers may have a hard time seeing themselves as leaders. Lead a discussion and give examples for inclusion, compassion, and compromise. Use leadership vocabulary. Help readers start to identify leadership traits in themselves. Introduce specific ideas about how to apply these traits at home.

TABLE OF CONTENTS

CHAPTER 1

WHAT IS LEADERSHIP?

Josh is learning about **recycling** at school. He wants to recycle more at home, so he makes a plan! His family joins him. Josh shows he is a leader at home.

Leadership is the ability to lead others. Leaders are people we want to follow. They have **traits** we want to show. Everyone can be a leader. You probably already are!

Being a leader isn't about telling people what to do. It's about helping and positively **influencing** those around you. It doesn't matter what you know or how old you are. Anyone can lead!

Who leads in your home? Is it your parents, grandparents, or guardians? These leaders care and provide for us. Older siblings are leaders, too. They can be good **role models**.

MANY TYPES OF HOUSEHOLDS

Who lives in your home? Every household and family looks different and has different members. But they all have leaders!

CHAPTER 2

GROW LEADERSHIP AT HOME

Do you have special jobs or chores you already do in your home? That is great! You can do more! What can you do to help and show you care at home?

Max sets the table for dinner each day. His mother doesn't even have to ask him. Doing things without being asked is a form of leadership. It shows **initiative**.

You can take initiative for yourself, too. Think ahead! Do your homework without being asked. Then your parents don't have to worry that you did it. This also shows that you are **responsible**. Other kids in your household see the example you set, too!

Sam's grandma has trouble walking up and down the stairs. Sam helps her. Helping others is a form of **service**. It puts others' needs before your own. It is **rewarding** to take action and be of service to others!

Tia wants to plant a garden. She makes a plan. Then she follows through. Why? Because it is something she cares about. She takes responsibility for the tasks she wants to be involved in.

Tia really wants her garden to grow! It takes time and **patience**. She tends to it every day. She is willing to work and wait to see results.

GROW YOUR MIND

Your mind can grow just like a garden! What can you do to grow your mind? Learn from your mistakes. Keep trying after you fail. Take little steps toward a big **goal**. This will help you accomplish big things!

CHAPTER 3

BE A LEADER!

Min organizes a fun game night! She brings everyone together for fun. They play games every Saturday night. It becomes a new family **tradition**. Can you think of a creative way to lead at home?

You could try a new recipe! Or think of a way to eat more healthy foods. Share your ideas with your family. Gather their **feedback**. Then lead the way!

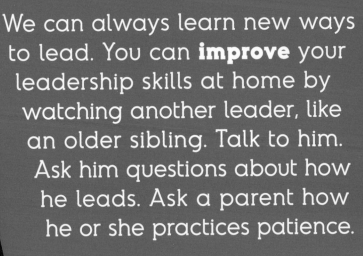

We can always learn new ways to lead. You can **improve** your leadership skills at home by watching another leader, like an older sibling. Talk to him. Ask him questions about how he leads. Ask a parent how he or she practices patience.

Being a leader can be hard. But it is rewarding. How can you lead at home?

ASK FOR FEEDBACK

Great leaders ask for feedback. You can give feedback, too. Feedback should be **specific**. It can tell someone what went well. Or it can suggest a way to improve. It can include ideas for change, too.

GOALS AND TOOLS

GROW WITH GOALS

Anyone can be a leader! By using leadership skills at home, you can develop leadership traits and be a leader everywhere you go!

Goal: Find a way to take initiative at home by doing helpful tasks. Write your ideas down. When you've finished, check those tasks off your list. Ask a parent or older sibling for some ideas of tasks you can do if you get stuck.

Goal: When you see a family member who needs help, ask how you can be of service. Step in if you know what to do. At dinner, ask an adult how they've showed service to others. Learn from their example.

Goal: Find a project at home that you can take responsibility for. Maybe you come up with the project. Or you can ask an adult for some ideas. Make a schedule so you don't forget!

WRITING REFLECTION

Practice seeing when you and others show leadership. Thinking about these actions and traits is one way that you will keep learning to be a leader.

1. Who have you seen take initiative in your home? What are ways you could take initiative at home?

2. Who practices service at your home? What are ways you practice service at home?

3. Have you seen someone else take responsibility for a project in your home? What are ways you could practice taking responsibility at home?

GLOSSARY

feedback
Written or spoken reactions to something that you are doing.

goal
Something you aim to do.

improve
To get better or make better.

influencing
Having an effect on someone or something.

initiative
The ability to take action without being told what to do.

patience
The ability to put up with problems or delays without getting angry or upset.

recycling
Processing old items, such as glass, plastic, or newspapers, so they can be used to make new products.

responsible
Able to be trusted.

rewarding
Offering or bringing satisfaction.

role models
People whose behaviors in certain areas are imitated by others.

service
Work that helps others.

specific
Precise, definite, or of a particular kind.

tradition
A custom, idea, or belief that is handed down from one generation to the next.

traits
Qualities or characteristics that make people different from each other.

TO LEARN MORE

FACT SURFER

Finding more information is as easy as 1, 2, 3.

1. Go to www.factsurfer.com

2. Enter "**leadershipathome**" into the search box.

3. Choose your cover to see a list of websites.

INDEX

Blue Owl Books are published by Jump!, 5357 Penn Avenue South, Minneapolis, MN 55419, www.jumplibrary.com

Copyright © 2020 Jump! International copyright reserved in all countries. No part of this book may be reproduced in any form without written permission from the publisher.

Library of Congress Cataloging-in-Publication Data

Names: Hancock, James, author.
Title: Leadership at home / by James Hancock.
Description: Blue owl books. | Minneapolis, MN: Jump!, [2020]
Series: Be a leader | Includes index. | Audience: Ages 7–10.
Identifiers: LCCN 2019032368 (print)
LCCN 2019032369 (ebook)
ISBN 9781645272267 (hardcover)
ISBN 9781645272274 (paperback)
ISBN 9781645272281 (ebook)
Subjects: LCSH: Leadership in children–Juvenile literature.
Leadership–Juvenile literature.
Classification: LCC BF723.L4 H36 2020 (print) | LCC BF723.L4 (ebook) | DDC 158/.4–dc23
LC record available at https://lccn.loc.gov/2019032368
LC ebook record available at https://lccn.loc.gov/2019032369

Editor: Susanne Bushman
Designer: Jenna Casura

Photo Credits: kate_sept2004/iStock, cover; Monkey Business Images/Shutterstock, 1; Phat1978/Shutterstock, 3; Tetra Images/Alamy, 4, 19; SDI Productions/iStock, 5; Comstock Images/Getty, 6–7; kirin_photo/iStock, 8–9; Sergey Novikov/Shutterstock, 10; Mint Images Limited/Alamy, 11; Firma V/Shutterstock, 12–13; Derek E. Rothchild/Getty, 14–15; Antonio_Diaz/iStock, 16–17; Mierya Acierto/Getty, 18; Image Source/iStock, 20–21.

Printed in the United States of America at Corporate Graphics in North Mankato, Minnesota.